Mommy Mine

by
Tim Warnes

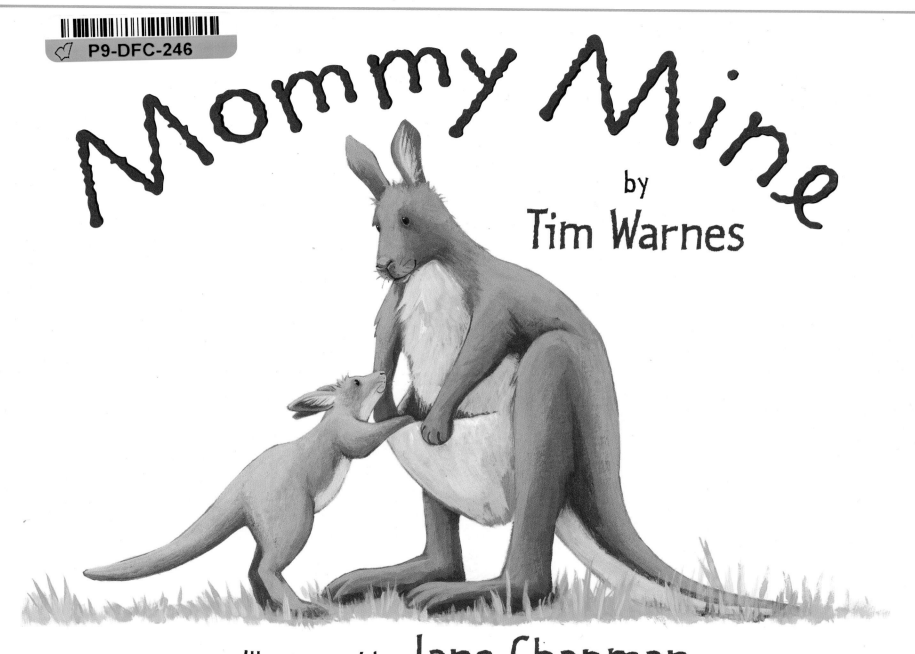

Illustrated by Jane Chapman

SCHOLASTIC INC.

New York Toronto London Auckland Sydney
Mexico City New Delhi Hong Kong Buenos Aires

ISBN 0-439-85272-2

Text copyright © 2005 by Tim Warnes.
Illustrations copyright © 2005 by Jane Chapman. All rights reserved.
Published by Scholastic Inc., 557 Broadway, New York, NY 10012,
by arrangement with HarperCollins Children's Books, a division of
HarperCollins Publishers Inc. SCHOLASTIC and associated logos are
trademarks and/or registered trademarks of Scholastic Inc.

12 11 10 9 8 7 6 5 4 3 2 1   6 7 8 9 10 11/0

Printed in the U.S.A.   08

First Scholastic printing, April 2006

Typography by Martha Rago

For Mummy Cuddles
— T.W., J.C.

Mommy **huge**

Mommy hairy

Mommy spiny

Mommy flutter

Mommy CHATTER

Mommy
tiny

pitter-patter

Mommy **LOUD**

Mommy STOMP

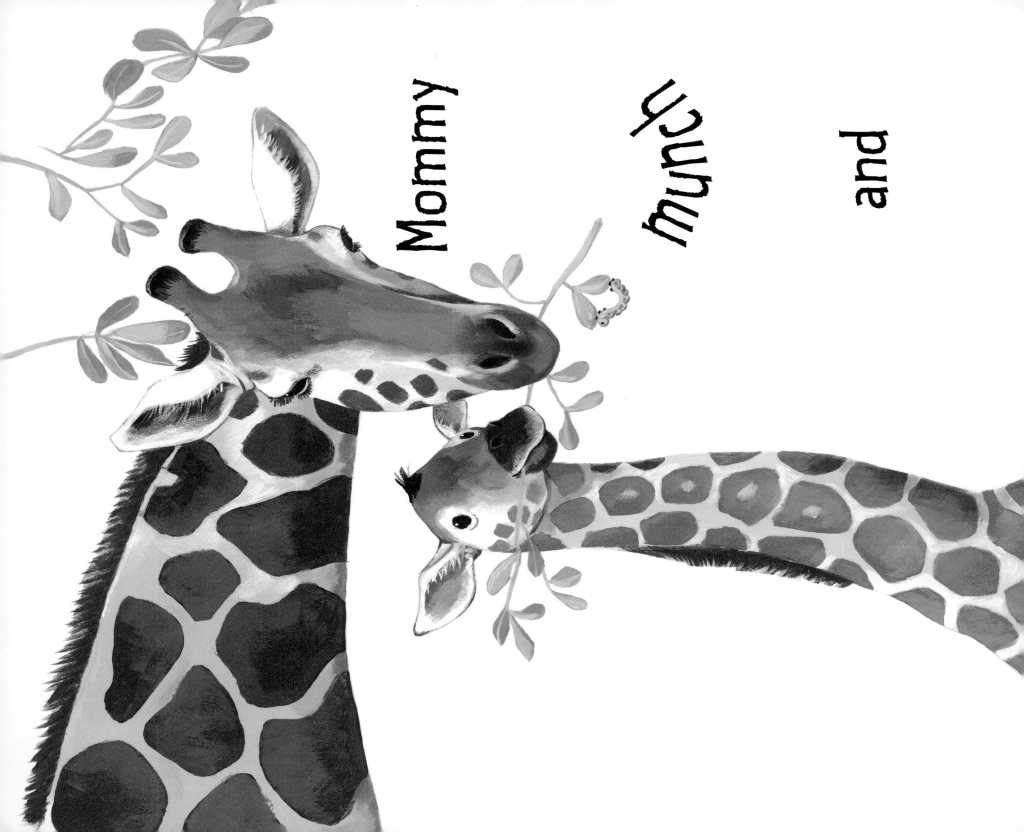

Mommy and munch

Mommy

chomp!

Mommy full Mommy grubby

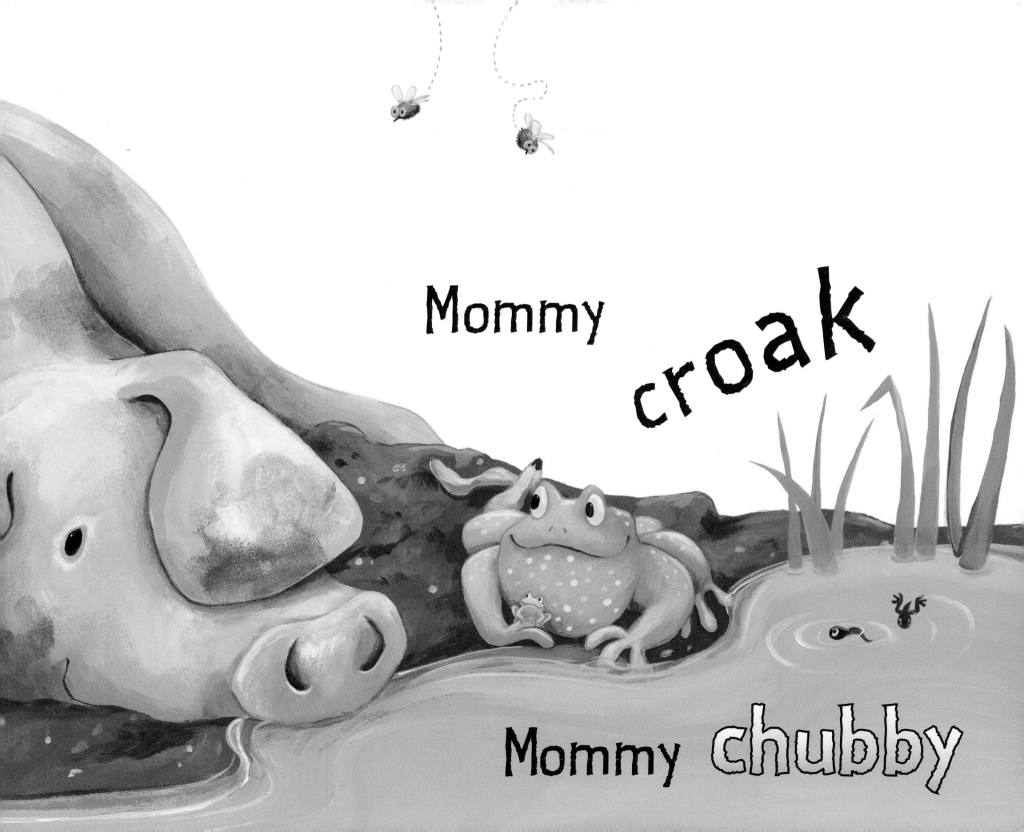

Mommy croak

Mommy chubby

Mommy jump

Mommy funny

Icky-sticky
Mommy
honey

Mommy snoozing, Mommy lazy

Mommy
noisy

Mommy
nosy

Mommy carry

Mommy
cozy.

Mommy cuddle on the vine,

Mommy kisses . . . .

Mommy mine!